this book belongs

to

_____

To my two
little
acorns and
one oak
tree. 🌰

Bala Kids
An imprint of Shambhala Publications, Inc.
2129 13th Street
Boulder, Colorado 80302
www.shambhala.com

Cover art and design: Betsy Petersen
Art Direction: Kara Plikaitis

9 8 7 6 5 4 3 2 1

First Edition
Printed in China

⊗ This edition is printed on acid-free paper that meets the American National
Standards Institute Z39.48 Standard.
♻ Shambhala makes every effort to print on postconsumer recycled paper.
For more information please visit www.shambhala.com.
Bala Kids is distributed worldwide by Penguin Random House, Inc., and its subsidiaries.

Library of Congress Cataloging-in-Publication Data
Names: Powers, Andie, author. | Petersen, Betsy, illustrator.
Title: I am quiet: a story for the introvert in all of us / Andie Powers;
illustrated by Betsy Petersen.
Description: First edition. | Boulder, Colorado: Bala Kids,
an imprint of Shambhala Publications, Inc, [2022]
Identifiers: LCCN 2020053489 | ISBN 9781611809848 (hardback)
Subjects: CYAC: Introversion—Fiction. | Quietude—Fiction. | Imagination—Fiction.
Classification: LCC PZ7.1.P3948 Iam 2022 | DDC [E]—dc23
LC record available at https://lccn.loc.gov/2020053489

I QUIET

A Story for the Introvert in All of Us

Andie Powers

illustrated by **Betsy Petersen**

bala kids

My name is Emile. I am quiet.
Grown-ups tell me, Don't be shy.

But I am not shy.

I AM QUIET.

I am quiet on the outside,
          but not on the inside.

On the inside,
     my imagination shouts loudly and runs wild.

On the inside,
I am Sir Emile, the valiant knight who roars louder than dragons. My armor clangs and clashes as I run with the mighty beasts. I high five the fiercest one and race to the finish line.

On the inside,

I am the daring captain of a great ship. I shout to my crew to pull up the anchor and onward we go! The waves thunder, spraying salty sea in my face. I salute the biggest whale and she joins my team.

But that is on the inside.

On the outside,
I build forts out of twigs that are secret spaces
for furry friends. I whisper about my day to them
and they tell me about theirs. Together we sneak
through mazes to look for tasty snacks.

On the outside,
I paint the universe on paper, and there is me,
floating through the stars. A tiny astronaut on a
great expedition that no one even knows about.
I paint a friend and we float together.

Some days I walk from home to school
through sun

or rain

or snow

and I listen to the sounds around me.

I hear quiet scuttling beneath the earth.
I see quiet nesting in the trees.
I feel quiet burrowing beneath the soil,
an oak tree growing deep in the ground until
it breaks free into the light, big and strong.

Strength can be quiet.

At school, Mae and Thomas are full of answers and ready to burst! I know the answers too, but I keep them like a secret. I whisper them to myself softly.

Answers can be quiet.

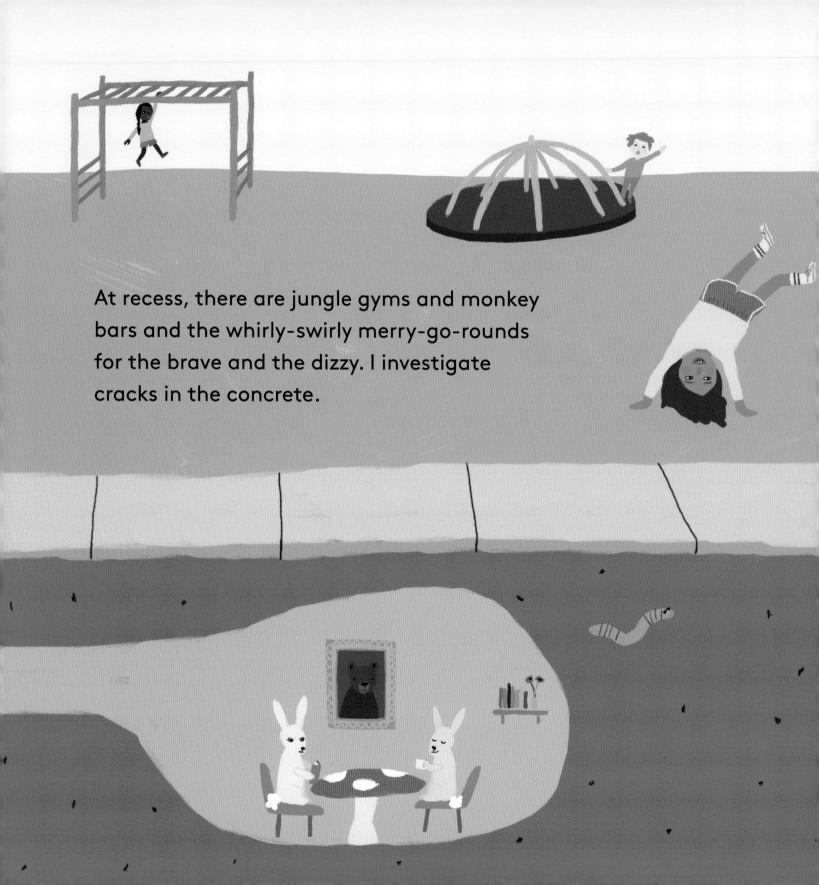

At recess, there are jungle gyms and monkey bars and the whirly-swirly merry-go-rounds for the brave and the dizzy. I investigate cracks in the concrete.

I look closely to see who I might find.
Sometimes I explore with a friend.

Friendship can be quiet.

On the way home from school, I pass our neighbors,
Mr. Tim and Bowser. Bowser is not quiet.
Bowser is loud, somehow without saying
much at all. Mr. Tim says,

Emile, don't be shy.

But I am not shy. I am quiet.
I show him so by barking back!

WOOF
WOOF!

Ms. Weero with her
noisy parakeet asks,
Cat got your tongue?

I stick out my tongue
and the parakeet does
too. Still there!

Mr. March in his rose
garden tells me,
Someday you will come
out of your shell.

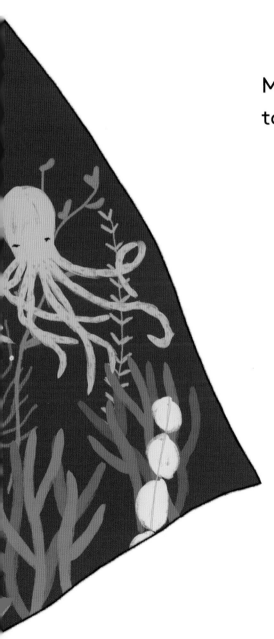

My mother says that if you hold a shell close
to your ear and

are

very

quiet,

you can hear the entire ocean sing.

At home, in bed, there are
snuggles and kisses and hugs,
then night-night.

My flashlight, books, and I have other plans.

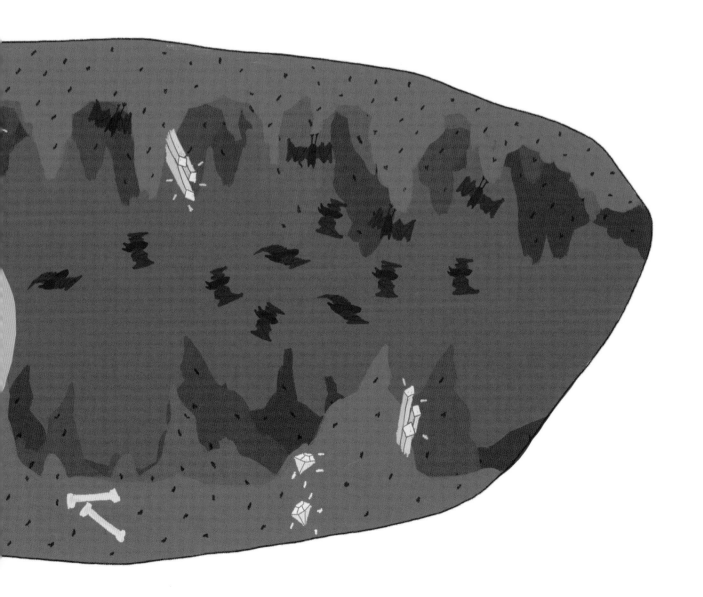

After miles of exploration, I click off the flashlight and snuggle in tight. I listen to the quiet sounds outside my window, close my eyes, and say good night.

AUTHOR'S note

When my daughter, Alice, was just one year old, I took her to a toddler music class. When we arrived, she ignored everyone in attendance and made a beeline for the giant Wurlitzer organ that sat in a corner. She quietly examined it while the other children played and squealed and banged instruments in a circle. After a few minutes, the instructor asked her if she would like to join the circle. She shook her head. "Don't be shy. It's okay," the instructor said. Alice didn't react and went back to examining the organ. As a former quiet kid myself, and now a happily introverted adult, I knew that Alice's silence had nothing to do with being timid or apprehensive. I remember the childhood feeling of grown-ups not fully seeing my true self. As a mother, I knew Alice to be a vibrant and bold yet ~~quiet~~ child. We didn't end up returning to the music class, but from that experience, Emile was born. Emile's story is for quiet kids who have felt misunderstood by grown-ups or categorized by someone who does not truly know them or their lively inner worlds. It's for the kid who prefers to read alone during recess or the kid who spends hours in the backyard, silently exploring. It's for the kid who is not shy, but quiet.